Welcome to Big Questions For Men 2022!
It's a book filled with life questions for you to go deep and find the answers that sit within you, without anyone's judgement.
The questions range from childhood dreams to relationships, money and career goals.There's extra lined pages should you be inspired to elaborate on your answers a little more, and some bonus graph paper if you want to get a little creative.
Enjoy!

May your life bring you all the blessings you desire.

L. Novoa

What did you dream of becoming when you were a child?

ACADEMIC/SPORTS/ARTISTIC?

WHY?

DID YOUR DREAM COME TRUE?

Something else you want to say?

DATE: __/__/____

What are relationship deal-breakers for you?

LIST IT

WHY?

DO YOU HAVE HIGH EXPECTATIONS?

Something else you want to say?

DATE: _ _ / _ _ / _ _ _ _

What makes you insecure?

MAKE A LIST

EXPLAIN

HOW DO YOU DEAL WITH IT?

Something else you want to say?

DATE: __/__/____

What have you done in your life that you're proud of?

CAREER/FAMILY/GOALS ACHIEVED?

WHY ARE YOU PROUD?

DID YOUR ACTIONS HELP OTHERS?

Something else you want to say?

DATE: __/__/____

What things make you angry?

ATTITUDES/LAZINESS/INJUSTICE?

WHY?

ANGER MANAGEMENT STRATEGY?

Something else you want to say?

DATE: __/__/____

What is a topic you can't shut up about?

WRITE IT OUT

WHY?

WHAT DO YOU WANT DO ABOUT IT?

Something else you want to say?

DATE: __/__/____

What would be a cause you would dedicate your life to?

WHO WOULD YOU HELP?

WHY?

CAN YOU START TOMORROW?

Something else you want to say?

DATE: __/__/____

Five words to describe your childhood.

LIST IT

WHY?

FAVOURITE MEMORY?

Something else you want to say?

What 3 events made the biggest impact on who you are today?

LIST IT

WHY?

WHAT DID YOU LEARN?

Something else you want to say?

DATE: __/__/____

What skill would you master if you had all the time in the world?

EG: LANGUAGE/INSTRUMENT?

WHY?

WHAT WOULD YOU DO WITH IT?

Something else you want to say?

DATE: __/__/____

Do you believe in a higher power?

WHAT?

WHY?

DO YOU HAVE 100% FAITH?

Something else you want to say?

Where in the world would you live if money wasn't an issue?

COUNTRY?

WHY?

WHAT ABOUT FAMILY/FRIENDS?

Something else you want to say?

DATE:__/__/____

What is your dream job?

LIST IT

WHY?

WILL YOU CHASE THIS DREAM?

Something else you want to say?

DATE: __/__/____

What is your stance on social media?

GOOD/BAD/INDIFFERENT

WHY?

COULD YOU LIVE WITHOUT IT?

Something else you want to say?

DATE: __/__/____

Who and what are you grateful for?

LIST IT

WHY?

DO YOU TELL THEM THAT YOU ARE?

Something else you want to say?

DATE: __/__/____

Who do you look up to?

LIST THEM

WHY?

WHAT HAVE YOU LEARNED?

Something else you want to say?

DATE: __/__/____

Would you ever go to a psychic or tarot card reader?

YES/NO/ALREADY DID

WHY?

WOULD YOU KEEP IT A SECRET?

Something else you want to say?

DATE: __/__/____

Do you think you're a good role model?

YES/NO/MAYBE

TO WHO?

DO YOU LEAD BY EXAMPLE?

Something else you want to say?

DATE: __/__/____

Would you sign up to start a human colony on a new planet?

YES/NO/DEPENDS

WHY?

ARE YOU SCARED OR EXCITED?

Something else you want to say?

DATE: __/__/____

What are your future career goals?

WHERE ARE YOU IN 2 YEARS?

WHERE ARE YOU IN 5 YEARS?

WHERE ARE YOU IN 10 YEARS?

Something else you want to say?

DATE: __/__/____

What would you do if you inherited two million dollars?

SPEND IT/SAVE IT/INVEST IT?

HELP OUT FAMILY/FRIENDS?

WOULD YOU TELL ANYONE?

Something else you want to say?

DATE: _ _ / _ _ / _ _ _ _

What's the nicest thing you've ever heard about yourself?

ELABORATE

HOW DID IT MAKE YOU FEEL?

DO YOU GIVE COMPLIMENTS?

Something else you want to say?

DATE:__/__/____

Who or what has completely lost your respect?

NAME OR DESCRIBE

WHY?

DO YOU FORGIVE AND FORGET ?

Something else you want to say?

DATE:__/__/____

What do you want to be remembered for after you die?

WHAT'S YOUR LEGACY?

____

____

____

____

____

WHY?

____

____

____

____

____

LAST WORDS OF ADVICE?

____

____

____

____

____

Something else you want to say?

You're done!

Keep this book and look back on it in a year. Reflect on your answers and see if things have changed. Maybe you would answer these questions differently the next time around. May your life bring you all the blessings you desire.

L. Novoa

www.ingramcontent.com/pod-product-compliance
Ingram Content Group UK Ltd.
Pitfield, Milton Keynes, MK11 3LW, UK
UKHW022011190726
13853UKWH00004B/1871